Ace of Spades

Paul Blum

RISING STARS

NASEN House, 4/5 Amber Business Village, Amber Close,
Amington, Tamworth, Staffordshire, B77 4RP

Rising Stars UK Ltd.
7 Hatchers Mews, Bermondsey Street, London SE1 3GS
www.risingstars-uk.com

Published 2012

Cover design: Burville-Riley Partnership
Brighton photographs: iStock
Illustrations: Chris King for Illustration Ltd (characters and cover artwork)/
Abigail Daker (map) http://illustratedmaps.info
Text design and typesetting: Geoff Rayner
Publisher: Rebecca Law
Editorial manager: Sasha Morton Creative Project Management

British Library Cataloguing in Publication Data.
A CIP record for this book is available from the British Library.

ISBN: 978-0-85769-603-8

Printed and bound by CPI Group (UK) Ltd, Croydon, CR0 4YY

Contents

Name:
John Logan

Age:
24

Hometown:
Manchester

Occupation:
Author of
supernatural
thrillers

Special skills:
Not yet known

profiles

Name:
Rose Petal

Age:
22

Hometown:
Brighton

Occupation:
Yoga teacher,
nightclub and
shop owner,
vampire hunter

Special skills:
Private investigator
specialising in
supernatural
crime

Location map

Brighton, East Sussex

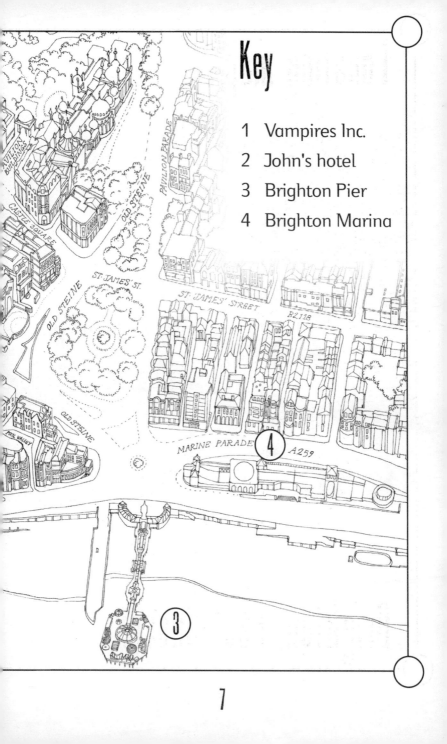

Key

1 Vampires Inc.
2 John's hotel
3 Brighton Pier
4 Brighton Marina

Chapter 1

David Cross pushed his way into the crowds of people. It was a busy Saturday in Brighton. There were tourists everywhere but he was still being followed. He saw Shorty Smith again. He knew he had to get out of sight.

David went with the flow of people walking along the pier. He walked into a noisy games arcade. Surely one man could disappear among all these people? Then he glanced up into a mirror and saw Shorty Smith looking back at him, grinning.

David was sweating. His heart beat faster and faster. Was his life going to end on this lovely sunny day at the seaside? He decided to hide out on the ghost train. Yet as soon as he took his seat, he saw the man in the ticket booth make a phone call. The gang controlled the funfair. The gang controlled everything in Brighton. David's ride was held up until Shorty had sat in the seat behind him. David jumped seats until he was sitting next to a girl who was dressed in black.

'Do you mind if I sit here?' he asked the girl, trying to smile. She looked away from him. She was probably as scared of him as he was of Shorty and the gang. Still, no one would dare attack him with a witness by his side.

When the ride was over, David spoke to the girl. 'Would you like to go for a cup of coffee?'

The girl smiled. 'I'm meeting a friend in half an hour. I suppose you could buy me a coffee first.'

'I know a nice place on the seafront,' David said. 'What's your name?'

'Mina,' she smiled again. 'What's yours?'

'I'm David Cross,' he replied, breathing a sigh of relief. While he was with someone, Shorty could not touch him. He half listened to Mina as she chatted to him.

'I work in a place called Vampires Inc.,' he heard her say. 'My friend, Rose, owns it. We teach yoga and it's a nightclub as well. You wouldn't believe how weird some of the customers are. We get all sorts, people who are into ghosts, zombies, vampires, werewolves . . .'

David smiled politely. 'I know more about vampires than you could ever dream,' he said to himself. But he was happy to let her talk. He needed as much time as he could get.

Just then, Mina looked at her watch. 'I've got to go now. It was nice to meet you, David,' she said. She stood up to leave and was surprised when David took her hand.

'Please, Mina, don't leave yet. I'm in trouble. Can I come with you?' he asked.

'What sort of trouble?' she replied.

'I can't say,' he said. 'Not yet, anyway.'

Mina frowned. 'Rose helps people in trouble. She might be able to help you.'

They left the café but a moment later Mina stopped walking. 'I've left my phone on the table. I must go back and get it.' She saw the look of fear in David's eyes. 'It's okay, just wait here, I'll be really quick,' she said.

Mina was only gone for two minutes. When she returned, she found a crowd of people standing where David had been. She pushed through them and found him lying on the ground. He was dying.

'They found me,' he whispered.

'Who found you?' Mina cried, taking his hand. But David did not reply. She looked down and saw that he was holding something. It was a playing card – the ace of spades. Turning it over she read what was written on the back of the card. Mina's eyes widened. She slipped the card into her bag and ran from the crowd without looking back. She had to get to Rose.

Chapter 2

At Vampires Inc., Rose's white owl,
Danny, sat on the bookshelf and looked
at Mina with his big green eyes. Mina
was sobbing. 'He was so frightened,
Rose. Who would have wanted to kill
him?'

'I'll speak to some of my contacts,'
said Rose. She was thinking about who
might be able to help her. As David's
murder wasn't supernatural, the police
wouldn't ask for her help. Rose was on
her own with this.

'Do you think I should have stayed
to tell the police what I knew?' Mina
whispered.

Rose looked at the playing card. The writing on the back was neat and clear. 'No,' she said. 'You did the right thing in bringing this straight to me.'

Vampires in trouble. Locked up. Help them.

John Logan was having a day off from his writing work. His research assistant, Rose Petal, had been seeing her friend Mina. So John decided to visit his mates in London. He was on the train back to Brighton when his phone rang. It was Rose.

'John, there's been a murder in the centre of Brighton,' she said. 'It was somebody Mina knows. There's something very odd about it. We need to talk.'

Another murder! John had learned quickly that working with Rose meant he saw a lot of dead bodies. She investigated supernatural crimes, he wrote books about them. They hadn't been working together for long, but they made a good team.

'I'll come straight to the club,' said John. 'See you in about an hour.'

****

Later that evening, Rose and John knew a lot more about David Cross. Rose had been staring at her computer screen for the whole afternoon, chasing leads and checking facts. Her eyes were red and aching when she stopped to sum up what they had found out.

'Okay, we know that David Cross was a professional gambler. He had just won a lot of money at Shorty Smith's casino in town. Shorty runs everything from the funfair to the chip shops. The police will think this case is a gangland killing. You don't go winning that much money from Shorty and get away with it.'

'So how is David Cross involved with vampires?' asked John, scratching his head. 'And what does the message on the back of the playing card mean?'

He saw Rose's face go pale. 'It seems that the front of the card is part of the message too. My contact in the police heard a rumour that some of my customers have left Brighton lately. They've gone to work on something called the Ace of Spades project,' she said.

'What kind of project is it?' asked John. He didn't like the sound of it.

'A top secret one. We think it's a fitness project. It tests how much stronger and faster vampires are than humans, and why,' she said. 'But none of the vampires who have worked on it has been seen or heard of again.'

'So what does this have to do with a dead card player, who won money in Brighton from the local gang leader?' said Logan.

'Let me dig around a bit,' Rose replied. 'We can talk later when I know more.'

22

Chapter 3

The next morning, John turned on his laptop. An email pinged up from Rose Petal.

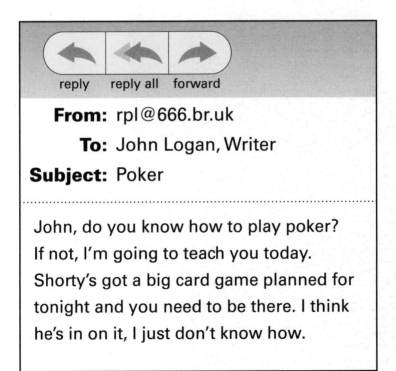

reply   reply all   forward

From: rpl@666.br.uk

To: John Logan, Writer

Subject: Poker

John, do you know how to play poker? If not, I'm going to teach you today. Shorty's got a big card game planned for tonight and you need to be there. I think he's in on it, I just don't know how.

John went to his hotel room window and looked at the waves crashing on the beach. It was a windy day. The sea was nervous and restless. He had a bad feeling about Rose's plan. A storm was coming.

****

'You're hopeless at this,' said Rose, putting down the cards again.

'Can't we just play another game of snap?' Logan sighed. 'I understand the rules for that.'

'Logan, you can't play snap when you go undercover,' she said grumpily. 'It's not going to impress your fellow card players. Let's start again.'

It was ten o'clock at night when a sleek, black car arrived at John's hotel to take him to the card game. The car was driven by a friend of Rose's, who worked for a rich vampire. The vampire's daughter had gone missing. She had agreed to take part in the Ace of Spades project two months ago and hadn't been seen since. A briefcase holding £10,000 was at John's feet. Rodney, the half werewolf fortune-teller, had even lent John a smart suit.

The card game was being held at Shorty Smith's home, a luxury flat on Brighton Marina.

'Make sure you impress Shorty with the way you play the game,' said Rose.

'If he likes you, he will talk about his business. If you lose money to him, he'll like you even more!'

'Cheers, Rose. Look, are you sure this spy camera will work?' asked John, tapping a small button on the briefcase. He was very nervous.

'It's never failed me yet,' smiled Rose. Sending John into a gangster's home to spy on him was a big risk. She waved John off and checked the web link to the camera worked. From her laptop, she could see everything the camera saw, but she was worried about John too.

Logan looked around the marina. The boat outside Shorty's flat was the biggest and most expensive of all. The driver told John he'd be waiting outside all night. The game was about to begin.

Chapter 4

'Welcome, Mr Logan,' said Shorty Smith. 'We always like to have new players at the table. I don't read much, but I hear you're a writer?'

John nodded and smiled nervously. There were two other players as well as Shorty. Each had put a large pile of money on the table. Both the men were tall, broad and silent. John started to sweat slightly. He added his cash to the table and set the briefcase on a nearby shelf. John made sure the camera was facing the players. He just hoped Rose could see everything.

The first half hour of the game went badly. Logan put all the wrong cards down at the wrong time. The other players looked surprised, but they were happy to take his money.

'I think I'll take a toilet break,' he said, looking at what little was left of his money.

Shorty showed him the way to the bathroom and went back to the game. The gangster's office was nearby. John quickly used the camera on his phone to snap photos of the papers on Shorty's desk. The computer was locked, but a small video camera lay on the desk, so John put it in his pocket. Hopefully, while John was out of the room, Rose would hear the rest of the gamblers say something useful. He waited for the phone in his pocket to vibrate. This would be the signal that Rose had got some information and he could leave.

Half an hour passed. John had run out of money.

'You're not much good at this, Mr Logan,' said Shorty Smith with a grin. 'Have you ever played cards before?'

Logan tried to smile as he scratched his ear. This was the signal to Rose he was going to get out of there. 'Perhaps I'm not as good as I thought. I think I'll leave you boys to it.'

'Some people would say you have more money than sense. I'm sure you have your reasons for being here tonight.' Shorty gave Logan a long hard stare.

'I'm better at snap,' said Logan. 'I've got fast reactions.'

'You'll need fast reactions if you're trying to trick me, son.'

John tried to stop his voice from shaking. 'Mr Smith, I'm going.' As he jumped up from his chair, the other two gamblers stood up too. John bumped into the table and Shorty's video camera fell out of his pocket. Now he really was in trouble.

Shorty snapped his fingers and the other two men started to reach for John. The lights in the room went out and the men began to twitch slightly. John looked at the door, but the men blocked his view. Suddenly he realised they were changing before his eyes. The twitching became shaking, and they grew taller and seemed scaly. How could this be happening?

There was only one way out. John threw himself under the table and scrambled between the chair legs. He headed for the door while the creatures continued to shake and change. Shorty Smith had gone. The other men seemed to have grown silver scales and huge, spiked tails. The floor was slippery as John crawled across the dark room. The door was locked!

Shrill screams came from the creatures and John realised they were shape-shifters. They could change form from humans to supernatural beings. He had to get out fast. Just as a clawed hand scratched at his arm, John saw an open window. He leapt through it and fell onto a balcony two floors below. From there, it was a small jump to the pavement. His driver revved the engine and John staggered into the back of the car. The driver locked the doors and roared off. Panting and bleeding from the jump, John tried to catch his breath. Finally, he looked up and saw who was driving. It was Shorty Smith!

Chapter 5

Shorty drove fast. The car flew out of the marina and away from the city. John tried to get the doors open but once again, he was trapped. A glass screen separated him from Shorty. John tried to phone Rose, but his handset was broken after the fall from the window. Looking out of the back of the car, he could see silvery shadows following them along the deserted beach. It was the creatures from the game. Shorty was leading them out to somewhere quiet so they could kill John. Unless Rose could track him down first.

Shorty drove down a dirt track into a small, pebbly cove. There was no moon over the water and it was pitch-black. The car screeched to a halt and John was dragged out of the back seat. Lying on the ground, Shorty held him down by the throat. He could hardly breathe. Behind Shorty, John could see that the shape-shifting creatures were going to catch up with them at any moment.

John heard fast, heavy footsteps on the pebbles. His heart was pounding but he managed to grab a rock and smash it against Shorty's leg. The gangster let out a yell of pain and John twisted out of his grip. He tripped and fell again onto the rocky ground. The creatures were nearly on top of him. John headed for the sea but one of the shape-shifters grabbed his shoulders in its slimy claws. John fell to the ground again and hit his head. He couldn't move.

Suddenly, John heard wings flapping and a high-pitched screech. Something was whirling around in the darkness, attacking the creatures. It was Rose's owl, Danny! He dived again and again, pecking at the creatures' eyes with his sharp beak. Danny was too quick for them to catch him, and soon both the shape-shifters were blinded. They stumbled, shrieking, into the sea. With a flick of their strong, spiked tails, they slid under the water and swam away. It was over.

****

John woke up in the hospital. Rose Petal was at his side.

'Danny saved my life,' he said. 'Did you send him?'

Rose squeezed his hand. 'Rodney and I saw everything on the video camera. While the shape-shifters changed form, Shorty found your driver and knocked him out. Rodney sensed where Shorty was taking you and we sent Danny on ahead. Rodney took care of Shorty. He won't be back in town for a while.'

'Everything hurts,' said John, feeling his head through the bandages. 'I hope it was worth it. What did you find out from the game?'

'Someone is taking our vampires and training them to kill in new and savage ways,' she said. 'These vampires are a new weapon. They are kept in cages behind bars and fed drugged blood. David Cross tried to explain what he saw on that card before he died.'

'So he was killed because he knew

too much,' said Logan rubbing his sore head. 'But I thought he was just a card player?'

'It turns out he was no more a card player than you,' she said. 'He was a scientist who worked on the project. I think he realised it wasn't just a research project. I think the vampires are going to be used as a weapon against humans. Now it's up to us to stop it. Are you in?'

John nodded slowly. Things were never what they seemed. But he wasn't going to let Rose stop the project alone. He was in – and in deep.

Glossary

ace of spades – the highest value playing card in the suit of spades

deserted – when a place is empty and there are no people

luxury – expensive

poker – a card game

professional gambler – a person who plays cards for money

undercover – when an ordinary person pretends to be a criminal so they can find out more about what the criminals are doing

witness – somebody who can tell the police what happened

zombies – dead human beings who come back to life

Quiz

1 Which fairground ride does David Cross go on to escape from the person who is following him?

2 Who is after him?

3 Why does Mina leave David on his own for two minutes?

4 What does David give to Mina as he dies?

5 Which card game does John Logan have to learn?

6 Which card game does he prefer playing?

7 What does John take with him to spy on the other card players?

8 What happens to the other card players after they start twitching?

9 Who saves John Logan's life?

10 What do Rose and John find out about the the Ace of Spades project?

Quiz answers

1 The ghost train

2 Shorty Smith

3 She left her phone in the café

4 The ace of spades playing card

5 Poker

6 Snap

7 A video camera attached to his briefcase

8 They shape-shift into monsters

9 Danny, the owl

10 Vampires are being fed with drugged blood and trained to kill humans

About the author

The author of these books teaches in a London school. At the weekend, his research takes him to the beaches and back streets of Brighton in search of werewolves and vampires.

He writes about what he has found.